JUV/E8
FIC
GANTOS

EASTSI

W9-AGV-507

R0404751348

Practice makes perfect for Rotten Ralph

DISCARD

DISCARD

CHICAGO PUBLIC LIBRARY
VODAK EASTSIDE BRANCH
3710 EAST 106 STREET
CHICAGO, IL 60617

Practice Makes Perfect for
ROTTEN RALPH

Written by **Jack Gantos**

Illustrated by **Nicole Rubel**

Farrar Straus Giroux

New York

For Mabel Grace —J.G.

For my family —N.R.

Text copyright © 2002 by Jack Gantos
Illustrations copyright © 2002 by Nicole Rubel
All rights reserved
Distributed in Canada by Douglas & McIntyre Ltd.
Color separations by Hong Kong Scanner Arts
Printed and bound in the United States of America by Berryville Graphics
Designed by Filomena Tuosto
First edition, 2002
3 5 7 9 10 8 6 4

Library of Congress Cataloging-in-Publication Data
Gantos, Jack.
  Practice makes perfect for Rotten Ralph / written by Jack Gantos ;
illustrated by Nicole Rubel.— 1st ed.
    p.   cm.
  Summary: When he goes to a carnival with Sarah and his cousin Percy,
Rotten Ralph learns that winning is not everything.
  ISBN 0-374-36356-0
  [1. Cats—Fiction. 2. Carnivals—Fiction. 3. Cheating—Fiction.] I. Rubel,
Nicole, ill. II. Title.

PZ7.G15334 Pr 2002
[E]—dc21

                                              2001023925

EAS

R0404751348

Contents

Everybody Loves a Winner · 7

Let the Games Begin · 15

A Cheater Prospers · 27

The Come-Back Cat · 35

Chicago Public Library
Vodak/East Side Branch
3710 E. 106th St.
Chicago, IL 60617

Everybody Loves a Winner

Rotten Ralph and Sarah were on their way to visit cousin Percy when they saw a new billboard.

"Look," said Sarah. "The carnival is coming to town."

I love to ride the bumper cars, thought Ralph.

"I love to eat cotton candy," said Sarah.

But most of all, Ralph said to himself, I love to play games and win *prizes*.

When they arrived at his house, Percy was busy throwing balls at a stack of cans.

"The carnival starts tonight and I've been practicing all morning," Percy said to Ralph.

"Well, I don't need to practice," Ralph replied. "I'm a natural at knocking things over."

"Ralph, I think practicing is a very good idea," said Sarah.

Percy smiled. "That's right, Ralph. Practice makes perfect."

Rotten Ralph yawned.

"Practice makes me tired," he said.

"Wake me up when it's time to go to the carnival."

While Rotten Ralph took a nap, Percy got himself ready. He smoothed his hair with mouse mousse. He cleaned the smudges off his glasses. He put on his lucky T-shirt. He tied a yellow ribbon around his neck.

"I sure wish Ralph would follow your fine example," Sarah said.

Yes, thought Percy. Ralph would be much improved if he were exactly like me.

Let the Games Begin

"Step right up!" shouted the carnival barker when he saw Ralph and Percy. "Try your luck throwing darts at balloons and win big prizes."

"I can win this kitty game with one eye closed," boasted Ralph.

He threw a dart. It hit a clown on his rubber nose. He threw another. It poked a hole in a kid's soda cup. His last throw was so wild, he didn't see where it went.

"My turn," said Percy. He took
careful aim and threw the darts. He
popped three balloons, and won a big
stuffed mouse.

"This is for you," he said, giving his prize to Sarah.

"Oh, Percy," cried Sarah. "All that practice really paid off."

At the beanbag toss, Ralph wouldn't
listen to Percy's advice.

"Suit yourself," sniffed his cousin.

Ralph missed all his shots.

"Watch me carefully, Ralph," said
Percy. "It's all in the wrist."

He made three shots in a row, and
won another fancy prize for Sarah.

At the "Test Your Strength" booth, Ralph picked up the sledgehammer. Now, this is something I should win, he decided as he flexed his muscles.

He hit the target. The meter barely moved. Ralph groaned weakly.

King
Kong
Kitty

Macho
Kitty

Mr.
Muscles

"Let me show you how it's done,"
said Percy.

He pounded the target with all his
might and rang the bell on top.

"Now, that is one super cat," said the
barker. "You win a King Kong Kitty."

Lovely
Lola
the
Snake Girl

Elmo
the
Flaming
Fire-eater

Slimy
Sam
the
Octopus
Boy

At the photo booth, Ralph was feeling fed up with Percy's winning ways. He refused to smile.

"Don't be a sourpuss, Ralph," Percy scolded.

"That's right, Ralph," said Sarah. "Winning isn't everything. Don't you agree, Percy?"

"I wouldn't know," Percy replied. "I always get what I aim for."

A Cheater Prospers

"Winning all these prizes has made me hungry," announced Percy. "We must get some nourishment."

But Ralph was hungry for prizes, not food.

"Okay, Ralph," Sarah said. "While Percy and I get a snack, why don't you keep playing. Remember, if at first you don't succeed, try, try again."

Ralph tried his luck at a guessing
game. He guessed wrong.

He tried to toss Ping-Pong balls into
fishbowls. But the balls bounced away.

Ralph was tired of losing. Next time, he thought, I will give myself a little extra help. The kind of sneaky help when nobody is looking.

When he rode the carousel, he used a sticky candy apple to snag the brass ring.

He won a stuffed shark.

"This is more like it," he said.

At the target-practice game, he
squirted the owner in the eyes, then
knocked over all the targets by hand.

He won a stuffed elephant.

Sarah will love this prize, he thought.

Then Ralph cheated at the go-cart
races. At the starting line, he popped
everyone's tires with his claws. He won
a giant trophy for coming in first.

Ralph held the trophy above his head. "I love winning prizes!" he shouted. "And Sarah loves a winner!"

The Come-Back Cat

When Sarah returned with Percy, she found Ralph staggering under the weight of all his prizes.

"These are for you," Ralph said.

"Goodness, Ralph!" Sarah cried. "How did you win all these prizes?"

Ralph didn't answer.

"Did you play fair and square?"

Ralph hung his head.

"Oh, for shame!" cried Percy.

"You know what you have to do now," Sarah said.

Ralph knew.

While Sarah looked after Percy,
Ralph returned the stuffed shark to the
carousel.

"I'm sorry I cheated a little," he said.

"Buster, there is no such thing as a
little cheating!" said the woman. She
kept the shark.

Then he returned the stuffed
elephant to the target-practice owner.

"Sorry," Ralph said. "I just got
carried away."

"Happens to the best of us," said the
man. Then he squirted Ralph in the
face.

Finally, Ralph dragged the trophy over to the racetrack.

"This belongs to you," he said to the owner.

The man made Ralph fix all his flat tires.

"Come back when you are ready to follow the rules," he said.

While Ralph waited for Percy and
Sarah to catch up to him, he practiced
throwing pennies in the wishing well:

40

"I wish I could win . . . I wish I could
win . . . I wish Sarah wouldn't think
Percy was so good at everything."

When Sarah found him, she was
smiling. "Ralph, I'm very proud of you
for telling the truth," she said. "Now
let's go home."

But Ralph wanted one more chance
to play fair and square. He smiled a
rotten smile at Percy and pointed to
the dunking booth.

"Oh, Ralph," said Percy. "You are a glutton for punishment. This really isn't fair, since I'm so much better than you."

"Then prove it," said Ralph. He climbed out onto the dunking seat.

But Percy was pooped after his big day. He missed all three times.

Then it was Ralph's turn to throw.

"If I can't do it," said Percy, "you *never* will." He bet his King Kong Kitty that Ralph would miss.

That was just what Ralph wanted. He took careful aim. He tossed a perfect throw. *Splash!* He dunked Percy on his first try.

"Help!" sputtered Percy.

"Time to practice your swimming," suggested Ralph.

Now he had two prizes, the King Kong Kitty and a stuffed animal from the dunking booth.

Rotten Ralph gave both his prizes to Sarah.

"Oh, Ralphie," she said. "You don't need any practice at being my winner." She gave him a big hug.

And after Sarah dried Percy off, they all went home.